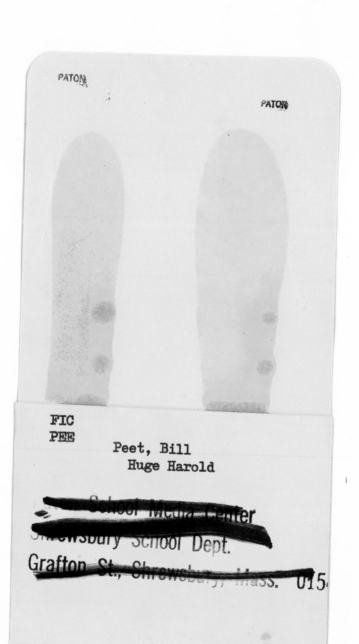

HUGE
HAROLD

Written and Illustrated by

BILL PEET

Houghton Mifflin Company Boston

When Harold the rabbit was tiny and small
His feet started growing and that's about all.
"Oh gracious!" his mother exclaimed in surprise.
"They're two times too big for a rabbit your size!"
"That's a sign," said his father, "he'll grow to great height."
And Father's prediction turned out to be right.

For Harold began to get bigger each day,
He grew all around and in every which way.
"Please!" cried his mother, "Stop growing right now!
Please, Harold, you're nearly as big as a cow!"

"Oh what a big problem!" his poor father cried.
"There's no place around here where Harold can hide.
He can't hide in bushes or in hollow logs,
He'll soon be discovered by hunters and dogs."
"That's right," his poor mother wailed in despair,
"He'll have to go live in a deep woods somewhere."

So with tears in their eyes the first thing the next day
They watched as huge Harold, their son, hopped away.
He galloped along on his big rabbit feet
Off through a meadow of waving gold wheat.
He crossed a green pasture without being seen,
Then he followed a creek bed along a ravine.

He hopped through a cornfield, along a rail fence,
And came to a woods that was gloomy and dense.
"I must say," said Harold, "it doesn't look cheery.
It looks very spooky and creepy and eery.
I suppose," he continued, "there's nothing to fear,
For it doesn't seem likely there's anyone here."

As he hopped down a path through the twisty old trees
There wasn't a sound but a whisper of breeze.
Then he heard a faint rustle—a twig-snapping sound—
And he stopped in his tracks to look quickly around.
He saw foxes and weasels with eyes black and beady
And a tree full of owls with eyes fierce and greedy.

"Now," said one owl, "if we play it just right
We'll all have a big rabbit banquet tonight."
"I'm sorry," said Harold, "to say I can't stay."
And in one frantic leap he was off and away.
He raced through the bushes at such a fast pace
That the weasels and foxes soon gave up the chase.
But Harold kept running, so great was his fright,
Till the spooky old forest was miles out of sight.

"I'm tired," said Harold, "I'm through for the day."
And he flopped down to rest on a big stack of hay.
But his nap was cut short by a bossy old cow,
Who said, "Get off our breakfast, and get out right now!"

"And stay out of my pen and don't eat in my trough,"
Said a grimy old pig. "Now you'd better be off."
Of course there was nothing that Harold could say,
So he left the cow pasture and went on his way.

As he rambled along a sweet scent crossed the breeze,
The fresh green aroma of lettuce and peas.
A scarecrow stood by with his arms in the air
As if he might say, "Help yourself, I don't care."

But Harold had no more than started his feast
When he heard someone shouting, "Now stop it, you beast!"
A farmer came running across a barn lot,
Took aim with his rifle and fired a shot.
Harold had never been shot at before
And he raced on in panic for five miles or more.

Then he stopped at a creek and sat down on a rock
And tried to relax and get over the shock.
"A big rabbit like me isn't safe anywhere,"
He said with a long weary sigh of despair.
As he sat staring helplessly down at his toes
A raindrop surprisingly plopped on his nose.

Wind whipped the cattails and stirred up the creek,
Lightning shot through the sky in a long jagged streak.
"It's a storm," said poor Harold, "I'd better find shelter."
And away to a hilltop he ran helter-skelter.

He discovered a house, a deserted old place
With dark ghostly windows like eyes on its face.
He approached the old mansion with feelings of doubt.
Which would be safer now, inside or out?
His decision was made by a great thunder crash
And Harold was through the front door in a flash.

He soon scrambled under a stairway to hide
And there he remained while the storm raged outside.
Thunder shook the old house till its dry timbers creaked,
Lightning flashed in the windows; the wind howled and shrieked.
Through the whole afternoon the storm raged on and on
But finally it ran out of breath and was gone.

Then Harold crawled out and began to explore.
He crept up the stairs to the very top floor,
Which was stacked to the rafters with all sorts of things
Including a bed with a mattress and springs.
He tried out the bed and he found it too small,
"But it's better," he reasoned, "than no bed at all."

He awoke the next day to the squeak of a door
And the sound of some footsteps below on the floor.
So he tiptoed downstairs to see what made the noise
And came face to face with two terrified boys.
"It's a ghost! It's a ghost!" they both screamed as they fled,
But one of them stopped. "It's a rabbit!" he said.
"Yes, that's the big rabbit that Oliver Hatch
Shot at and missed in his vegetable patch."
And away they both ran just as fast as they could
To tell everyone in the whole neighborhood.

The farmers stopped plowing and started right out
To hunt the big rabbit they'd all heard about.
When they reached the old mansion no rabbit was there,
He was racing far off through the country somewhere.
But the hunters kept snooping and picked up the trail
And they started the hunt for the big cottontail.

Huge Harold was now in a worse spot than ever,
To outwit the hunters he'd have to be clever.
He ran down ravines and he ran up low ridges
And waded down creeks and he hid under bridges.
He ran on for many and many a mile,
Then finally decided to rest for a while.

So he spotted a hide-out and with a big hop
He came plopping down in a leafy treetop.
This fooled the hunters and also their dogs,
Who sniffed round the tree trunk and peeked into logs,
But they never once thought to look up in the tree.
It wasn't a place where a rabbit should be.
So at last they gave up and all went away
And promised to start again early next day.

The great hunt continued for week after week,
Like a countryside contest of hide-and-go-seek.
It went on and on through the month of September
And into October and all through November.
December arrived with the first heavy snow
And the temperature dropped down to fourteen below.

Harold shivered and shook from his frost-bitten nose
All the way down to his half-frozen toes.
"I'm done for," he said, "I'm through altogether,
If I don't get out of this terrible weather."

Just about then something red caught his eye,
A big friendly barn on a hilltop nearby.
He headed straight for it and in one big hop
He leaped through the window way up in the top.
Then he said as he lay in a big bed of hay,
"This is the end, I'm through running away."

Harold was spotted by Orville B. Croft,
Who heard some loud snoring way up in his loft.
"Well now," he said, "doggone and dagnabit!
That's what I call a whoppin' big rabbit!"
Then all at once he heard someone shout
And he opened a window and poked his head out.

"What's all the commotion and hullabaloo?
I'd just like to know what you think you're up to?"
"We're hunting a rabbit," the hunters replied,
"And we'll look through your barn if you'll let us inside."
"He's in here," said Orville, "and here's where he'll stay
And you're not coming in, so be off on your way."
The hunters all grumbled and kicked up the snow
But at last they gave up and decided to go.

Orville B. Croft was both gentle and kind,
But still Harold feared what he might have in mind.
He was given fresh water and always well fed,
Along with the horses, both Buster and Ted.
"I know," thought Harold, "just what he's up to,
He'll fatten me up for a big rabbit stew."

But when winter was over and spring came along
Harold discovered that he had been wrong.
One day he was brushed with the greatest of care
To get all the foxtails and burs from his hair.

He was hitched to a buggy with harness and reins,
Then went trotting off down the back country lanes.
"Now this is more like it!" huge Harold said,
"I'm treated as well as a fine thoroughbred."

At the end of the summer he went to the fair
And created a lot of excitement while there.
The question came up as to whether or not
A rabbit could enter the championship trot.

They looked up the rules but they couldn't find one
That said, "It's not fair for a rabbit to run."
So he ran in the race and won going away
And became a champion trotter that day.

The crowd loved huge Harold and all brought him treats
Such as lettuce and celery, spinach and beets.
It was too good to be true, like a wonderful dream,
Why, they even brought Harold some carrot ice cream.
But all this success didn't go to his head,
He remained very modest and humble instead.
For rabbits you see aren't affected by fame,
No matter what happens they're always the same.